DENTS IN THE LIFE OF A SLAVE GIRL - PART I

HARRIET A. JACOBS

Made with ♥ on the Notion Press Platform
www.notionpress.com

Contents

Preface

Reader, be assured this narrative is no fiction. I am aware that some of my adventures may seem incredible; but they are, nevertheless, strictly true. I have not exaggerated the wrongs inflicted by Slavery; on the contrary, my descriptions fall far short of the facts. I have concealed the names of places, and given persons fictitious names. I had no motive for secrecy on my own account, but I deemed it kind and considerate towards others to pursue this course.

I wish I were more competent to the task I have undertaken. But I trust my readers will excuse deficiencies in consideration of circumstances. I was born and reared in Slavery; and I remained in a Slave State twenty-seven years. Since I have been at the North, it has been necessary for me to work diligently for my own support, and the education of my children. This has not left me much leisure to make up for the loss of early opportunities to improve myself; and it has compelled me to write these pages at irregular intervals, whenever I could snatch an hour from household duties.

When I first arrived in Philadelphia, Bishop Paine advised me to publish a sketch of my life, but I told him I was altogether incompetent to such an undertaking. Though I have improved my mind somewhat since that time, I still remain of the same opinion; but I trust my motives will excuse what might otherwise seem presumptuous. I have not written my experiences in order to attract attention to myself; on the contrary, it would have been more pleasant to me to have been silent about my own history. Neither do I care to excite sympathy for my own sufferings. But I do earnestly desire to arouse the women of the North to a realizing sense of the condition of two millions of women at the South, still in bondage, suffering what I suffered, and most of them far worse. I want to add my testimony to that of abler pens to convince the people of the Free States what Slavery really is. Only by experience can any one realize how deep, and dark, and foul is that pit of abominations. May the blessing of God rest on this imperfect effort in behalf of my persecuted people!

Introduction By The Editor

The author of the following autobiography is personally known to me, and her conversation and manners inspire me with confidence. During the last seventeen years, she has lived the greater part of the time with a distinguished family in New York, and has so deported herself as to be highly esteemed by them. This fact is sufficient, without further credentials of her character. I believe those who know her will not be disposed to doubt her veracity, though some incidents in her story are more romantic than fiction.

At her request, I have revised her manuscript; but such changes as I have made have been mainly for purposes of condensation and orderly arrangement. I have not added any thing to the incidents, or changed the import of her very pertinent remarks. With trifling exceptions, both the ideas and the language are her own. I pruned excrescences a little, but otherwise I had no reason for changing her lively and dramatic way of telling her own story. The names of both persons and places are known to me; but for good reasons I suppress them.

It will naturally excite surprise that a woman reared in Slavery should be able to write so well. But circumstances will explain this. In the first place, nature endowed her with quick perceptions. Secondly, the mistress, with whom she lived till she was twelve years old, was a kind, considerate friend, who taught her to read and spell. Thirdly, she was placed in favorable circumstances after she came to the North; having frequent intercourse with intelligent persons, who felt a friendly interest in her welfare, and were disposed to give her opportunities for self-improvement.

I am well aware that many will accuse me of indecorum for presenting these pages to the public; for the experiences of this intelligent and much-injured woman belong to a class which some call delicate subjects, and others indelicate. This peculiar phase of Slavery has generally been kept veiled; but the public ought to be made acquainted with its monstrous features, and I willingly take the responsibility of presenting them with the veil withdrawn. I do this for the sake of my sisters in bondage, who are suffering wrongs so foul, that our ears are too delicate to listen to them. I do it with the hope of arousing conscientious and reflecting women at the North to a sense of their duty in the exertion of moral influence on the question of Slavery, on all possible occasions. I do it with the hope that every man who reads this narrative will swear solemnly before God that, so far as he has power to prevent it, no fugitive from Slavery shall ever be sent back to suffer in that loathsome den of corruption and cruelty.

L. Maria Child.

INCIDENTS IN THE LIFE OF A SLAVE GIRL, SEVEN YEARS CONCEALED.

CHAPTER ONE

Childhood

I was born a slave; but I never knew it till six years of happy childhood had passed away. My father was a carpenter, and considered so intelligent and skilful in his trade, that, when buildings out of the common line were to be erected, he was sent for from long distances, to be head workman. On condition of paying his mistress two hundred dollars a year, and supporting himself, he was allowed to work at his trade, and manage his own affairs. His strongest wish was to purchase his children; but, though he several times offered his hard earnings for that purpose, he never succeeded. In complexion my parents were a light shade of brownish yellow, and were termed mulattoes. They lived together in a comfortable home; and, though we were all slaves, I was so fondly shielded that I never dreamed I was a piece of merchandise, trusted to them for safe keeping, and liable to be demanded of them at any moment. I had one brother, William, who was two years younger than myself—a bright, affectionate child. I had also a great treasure in my maternal grandmother, who was a remarkable woman in many respects. She was the daughter of a planter in South Carolina, who, at his death, left her mother and his three children free, with money to go to St. Augustine, where they had relatives. It was during the

Revolutionary War; and they were captured on their passage, carried back, and sold to different purchasers. Such was the story my grandmother used to tell me; but I do not remember all the particulars. She was a little girl when she was captured and sold to the keeper of a large hotel. I have often heard her tell how hard she fared during childhood. But as she grew older she evinced so much intelligence, and was so faithful, that her master and mistress could not help seeing it was for their interest to take care of such a valuable piece of property. She became an indispensable personage in the household, officiating in all capacities, from cook and wet nurse to seamstress. She was much praised for her cooking; and her nice crackers became so famous in the neighborhood that many people were desirous of obtaining them. In consequence of numerous requests of this kind, she asked permission of her mistress to bake crackers at night, after all the household work was done; and she obtained leave to do it, provided she would clothe herself and her children from the profits. Upon these terms, after working hard all day for her mistress, she began her midnight bakings, assisted by her two oldest children. The business proved profitable; and each year she laid by a little, which was saved for a fund to purchase her children. Her master died, and the property was divided among his heirs. The widow had her dower in the hotel, which she continued to keep open. My grandmother remained in her service as a slave; but her children were divided among her master's children. As she had five, Benjamin, the youngest one, was sold, in order that each heir might have an equal portion of dollars and cents. There was so little difference in our ages that he seemed more like my brother than my uncle. He was a bright, handsome lad, nearly white; for he inherited the complexion my grandmother had derived from Anglo-Saxon ancestors. Though only ten years old, seven hundred and twenty dollars were paid for him. His sale was a terrible blow to my grandmother; but she was naturally hopeful, and she went to work with renewed energy, trusting in time to be able to purchase some of her children. She had laid up three hundred dollars, which her mistress one day begged as a loan, promising to pay her soon. The reader probably knows that no promise or writing given to a slave is legally binding; for, according to Southern laws, a slave, being property, can hold no property. When my grandmother lent her hard earnings to her mistress, she trusted solely to her honor. The honor of a slaveholder to a slave!

To this good grandmother I was indebted for many comforts. My brother Willie and I often received portions of the crackers, cakes, and preserves, she made to sell; and after we ceased to be children we were indebted to her for many more important services.

Such were the unusually fortunate circumstances of my early childhood. When I was six years old, my mother died; and then, for the first time, I learned, by the talk around me, that I was a slave. My mother's mistress was the daughter of my grandmother's mistress. She was the foster sister of my mother; they were both nourished at my grandmother's breast. In fact, my mother had been weaned at three months old, that the babe of the mistress might obtain sufficient food. They played together as children; and, when they became women, my mother was a most faithful servant to her whiter foster sister. On her death-bed her mistress promised that her children should never suffer for any thing; and during her lifetime she kept her word. They all spoke kindly of my dead mother, who had been a slave merely in name, but in nature was noble and womanly. I grieved for her, and my young mind was troubled with the thought who would now take care of me and my little brother. I was told that my home was now to be with her mistress; and I found it a happy one. No toilsome or disagreeable duties were imposed upon me. My mistress was so kind to me that I was always glad to do her bidding, and proud to labor for her as much as my young years would permit. I would sit by her side for hours, sewing diligently, with a heart as free from care as that of any free-born white child. When she thought I was tired, she would send me out to run and jump; and away I bounded, to gather berries or flowers to decorate her room. Those were happy days—too happy to last. The slave child had no thought for the morrow; but there came that blight, which too surely waits on every human being born to be a chattel.

When I was nearly twelve years old, my kind mistress sickened and died. As I saw the cheek grow paler, and the eye more glassy, how earnestly I prayed in my heart that she might live! I loved her; for she had been almost like a mother to me. My prayers were not answered. She died, and they buried her in the little churchyard, where, day after day, my tears fell upon her grave.

I was sent to spend a week with my grandmother. I was now old enough to begin to think of the future; and again and again I asked myself what they would do with me. I felt sure I should never find another mistress so kind as the one who was gone. She had promised my dying mother that her children should never suffer for any thing; and when I remembered that, and recalled her many proofs of attachment to me, I could not help having some hopes that she had left me free. My friends were almost certain it would be so. They thought she would be sure to do it, on account of my mother's love and faithful service. But, alas! we all know that the memory of a faithful slave does not avail much to save her children from the auction block.

After a brief period of suspense, the will of my mistress was read, and we learned that she had bequeathed me to her sister's daughter, a child of five years old. So vanished our hopes. My mistress had taught me the precepts of God's Word: "Thou shalt love thy neighbor as thyself." "Whatsoever ye would that men should do unto you, do ye even so unto them." But I was her slave, and I suppose she did not recognize me as her neighbor. I would give much to blot out from my memory that one great wrong. As a child, I loved my mistress; and, looking back on the happy days I spent with her, I try to think with less bitterness of this act of injustice. While I was with her, she taught me to read and spell; and for this privilege, which so rarely falls to the lot of a slave, I bless her memory.

She possessed but few slaves; and at her death those were all distributed among her relatives. Five of them were my grandmother's children, and had shared the same milk that nourished her mother's children. Notwithstanding my grandmother's long and faithful service to her owners, not one of her children escaped the auction block. These God-breathing machines are no more, in the sight of their masters, than the cotton they plant, or the horses they tend.

The New Master And Mistress.

Dr. Flint, a physician in the neighborhood, had married the sister of my mistress, and I was now the property of their little daughter. It was not without murmuring that I prepared for my new home; and what added to my unhappiness, was the fact that my brother William was purchased by the same family. My father, by his nature, as well as by the habit of transacting business as a skilful mechanic, had more of the feelings of a freeman than is common among slaves. My brother was a spirited boy; and being brought up under such influences, he early detested the name of master and mistress. One day, when his father and his mistress both happened to call him at the same time, he hesitated between the two; being perplexed to know which had the strongest claim upon his obedience. He finally concluded to go to his mistress. When my father reproved him for it, he said, "You both called me, and I didn't know which I ought to go to first."

"You are my child," replied our father, "and when I call you, you should come immediately, if you have to pass through fire and water."

Poor Willie! He was now to learn his first lesson of obedience to a master. Grandmother tried to cheer us with hopeful words, and they found an echo in the credulous hearts of youth.

When we entered our new home we encountered cold looks, cold words, and cold treatment. We were glad when the night came. On my narrow bed I moaned and wept, I felt so desolate and alone.

I had been there nearly a year, when a dear little friend of mine was buried. I heard her mother sob, as the clods fell on the coffin of her only child, and I turned away from the grave, feeling thankful that I still had something left to love. I met my grandmother, who said, "Come with me, Linda;" and from her tone I knew that something sad had happened. She led me apart from the people, and then said, "My child, your father is dead." Dead! How could I believe it? He had died so suddenly I had not even heard that he was sick. I went home with my grandmother. My heart rebelled against God, who had taken from me mother, father, mistress, and friend. The good grandmother tried to comfort me. "Who knows the ways of God?" said she. "Perhaps they have been kindly taken from the evil days to come." Years afterwards I often thought of this. She promised to be a mother to her grandchildren, so far as she might be permitted to do so; and strengthened by her love, I returned to my master's. I thought I should be allowed to go to my father's house the next morning; but I was ordered to go for flowers, that my mistress's house might be decorated for an evening party. I spent the day gathering flowers and weaving them into festoons, while the dead body of my father was lying within a mile of me. What cared my owners for that? he was merely a piece of property. Moreover, they thought he had spoiled his children, by teaching them to feel that they were human beings. This was blasphemous doctrine for a slave to teach; presumptuous in him, and dangerous to the masters.

The next day I followed his remains to a humble grave beside that of my dear mother. There were those who knew my father's worth, and respected his memory.

My home now seemed more dreary than ever. The laugh of the little slave-children sounded harsh and cruel. It was selfish to feel so about the joy of others. My brother moved about with a very grave face. I tried to comfort him, by saying, "Take courage, Willie; brighter days will come by and by."

"You don't know any thing about it, Linda," he replied. "We shall have to stay here all our days; we shall never be free."

I argued that we were growing older and stronger, and that perhaps we might, before long, be allowed to hire our own time, and then we could earn money to buy our freedom. William declared this was much easier to say than to do; moreover, he did not intend to buy his freedom. We held daily controversies upon this subject.

Little attention was paid to the slaves' meals in Dr. Flint's house. If they could catch a bit of food while it was going, well and good. I gave myself no trouble on that score, for on my various errands I passed my grandmother's house, where there was always something to spare for me. I was frequently threatened with punishment if I stopped there; and my grandmother, to avoid detaining me, often stood at the gate with something for my breakfast or dinner. I was indebted to her for all my comforts, spiritual or temporal. It was her labor that supplied my scanty wardrobe. I have a vivid recollection of the linsey-woolsey dress given me every winter by Mrs. Flint. How I hated it!

It was one of the badges of slavery.

While my grandmother was thus helping to support me from her hard earnings, the three hundred dollars she had lent her mistress were never repaid. When her mistress died, her son-in-law, Dr. Flint, was appointed executor. When grandmother applied to him for payment, he said the estate was insolvent, and the law prohibited payment. It did not, however, prohibit him from retaining the silver candelabra, which had been purchased with that money. I presume they will be handed down in the family, from generation to generation.

My grandmother's mistress had always promised her that, at her death, she should be free; and it was said that in her will she made good the promise. But when the estate was settled, Dr. Flint told the faithful old servant that, under existing circumstances, it was necessary she should be sold.

On the appointed day, the customary advertisement was posted up, proclaiming that there would be a "public sale of negroes, horses, &c." Dr. Flint called to tell my grandmother that he was unwilling to wound her feelings by putting her up at auction, and that he would prefer to dispose of her at private sale. My grandmother saw through his hypocrisy; she understood very well that he was ashamed of the job. She was a very spirited woman, and if he was base enough to sell her, when her mistress intended she should be free, she was determined the public should know it. She had for a long time supplied many families with crackers and preserves; consequently, "Aunt Marthy," as she was called, was generally known, and every body who knew her respected her intelligence and good character. Her long and faithful service in the family was also well known, and the intention of her mistress to leave her free. When the day of sale came, she took her place among the chattels, and at the first call she sprang upon the auction-block. Many voices called out, "Shame! Shame! Who is going to sell you, aunt Marthy? Don't stand there! That is no place for you." Without saying a word, she quietly awaited her fate. No one bid for her. At last, a feeble voice said, "Fifty dollars." It came from a maiden lady, seventy years old, the sister of my grandmother's deceased mistress. She had lived forty years under the same roof with my grandmother; she knew how faithfully she had served her owners, and how cruelly she had been defrauded of her rights; and she resolved to protect her. The auctioneer waited for a higher bid; but her wishes were respected; no one bid above her. She could neither read nor write; and when the bill of sale was made out, she signed it with a cross. But what consequence was that, when she had a big heart overflowing with human kindness? She gave the old servant her freedom.

At that time, my grandmother was just fifty years old. Laborious years had passed since then; and now my brother and I were slaves to the man who had defrauded her of her money, and tried to defraud her of her freedom. One of my mother's sisters, called Aunt Nancy, was also a slave in his family. She was a kind, good aunt to me; and supplied the place of both housekeeper and waiting maid to her mistress. She was, in fact, at the beginning and end of every thing.

Mrs. Flint, like many southern women, was totally deficient in energy. She had not strength to superintend her household affairs; but her nerves were so strong, that she could sit in her easy chair and see a woman whipped, till the blood trickled from every stroke of the lash. She was a member of the church; but partaking of the Lord's supper did not seem to put her in a Christian frame of mind. If dinner was not served at the exact time on that particular Sunday, she would station herself in the kitchen, and wait till it was dished, and then spit in all the kettles and pans that had been used for cooking. She did this to prevent the cook and her children from eking out their meagre fare with the remains of the gravy and other scrapings. The slaves could get nothing to eat except what she chose to give them. Provisions were weighed out by the pound and ounce, three times a day. I can assure you she gave them no chance to eat wheat bread from her flour barrel. She knew how many biscuits a quart of flour would make, and exactly what size they ought to be.

Dr. Flint was an epicure. The cook never sent a dinner to his table without fear and trembling; for if there happened to be a dish not to his liking, he would either order her to be whipped, or compel her to eat every mouthful of it in his presence. The poor, hungry creature might not have objected to eating it; but she did object to having her master cram it down her throat till she choked.

They had a pet dog, that was a nuisance in the house. The cook was ordered to make some Indian mush for him. He refused to eat, and when his head was held over it, the froth flowed from his mouth into the basin. He died a few minutes after. When Dr. Flint came in, he said the mush had not been well cooked, and that was the reason the animal would not eat it. He sent for the cook, and compelled her to eat it. He thought that the woman's stomach was stronger than the dog's; but her sufferings afterwards proved that he was mistaken. This poor woman endured many cruelties from her master and mistress; sometimes she was locked up, away from her nursing baby, for a whole day and night.

When I had been in the family a few weeks, one of the plantation slaves was brought to town, by order of his master. It was near night when he arrived, and Dr. Flint ordered him to be taken to the work house, and tied up to the joist, so that his feet would just escape the ground. In that situation he was to wait till the doctor had taken his tea. I shall never forget that night. Never before, in my life, had I heard hundreds of blows fall, in succession, on a human being. His piteous groans, and his "O, pray don't, massa," rang in my ear for months afterwards. There were many conjectures as to the cause of this terrible punishment. Some said master accused him of stealing corn; others said the slave had quarrelled with his wife, in presence of the overseer, and had accused his master of being the father of her child. They were both black, and the child was very fair.

I went into the work house next morning, and saw the cowhide still wet with blood, and the boards all covered with gore. The poor man lived, and continued to quarrel with his wife. A few months afterwards Dr. Flint handed them both over to a slave-trader. The guilty man put their value into his pocket, and had the satisfaction of knowing that they were out of sight and hearing. When the mother was delivered into the trader's hands, she said, "You promised to treat me well." To which he replied, "You have let your tongue run too far; damn you!" She had forgotten that it was a crime for a slave to tell who was the father of her child.

From others than the master persecution also comes in such cases. I once saw a young slave girl dying soon after the birth of a child nearly white. In her agony she cried out, "O Lord, come and take me!" Her mistress stood by, and mocked at her like an incarnate fiend. "You suffer, do you?"

she exclaimed. "I am glad of it. You deserve it all, and more too."

The girl's mother said, "The baby is dead, thank God; and I hope my poor child will soon be in heaven, too."

"Heaven!" retorted the mistress. "There is no such place for the like of her and her bastard."

The poor mother turned away, sobbing. Her dying daughter called her, feebly, and as she bent over her, I heard her say, "Don't grieve so, mother; God knows all about it; and HE will have mercy upon me."

Her sufferings, afterwards, became so intense, that her mistress felt unable to stay; but when she left the room, the scornful smile was still on her lips. Seven children called her mother. The poor black woman had but the one child, whose eyes she saw closing in death, while she thanked God for taking her away from the greater bitterness of life.

CHAPTER THREE

The Slaves' New Year's Day.

Dr. Flint owned a fine residence in town, several farms, and about fifty slaves, besides hiring a number by the year.

Hiring-day at the south takes place on the 1st of January. On the 2d, the slaves are expected to go to their new masters. On a farm, they work until the corn and cotton are laid. They then have two holidays. Some masters give them a good dinner under the trees. This over, they work until Christmas eve. If no heavy charges are meantime brought against them, they are given four or five holidays, whichever the master or overseer may think proper. Then comes New Year's eve; and they gather together their little alls, or more properly speaking, their little nothings, and wait anxiously for the dawning of day. At the appointed hour the grounds are thronged with men, women, and children, waiting, like criminals, to hear their doom pronounced. The slave is sure to know who is the most humane, or cruel master, within forty miles of him.

It is easy to find out, on that day, who clothes and feeds his slaves well; for he is surrounded by a crowd, begging, "Please, massa, hire me this year. I will work very hard, massa."

If a slave is unwilling to go with his new master, he is whipped, or locked up in jail, until he consents to go, and promises not to run away during the year. Should he chance to change his mind, thinking it justifiable to violate an extorted promise, woe unto him if he is caught! The whip is used till the blood flows at his feet; and his stiffened limbs are put in chains, to be dragged in the field for days and days!

If he lives until the next year, perhaps the same man will hire him again, without even giving him an opportunity of going to the hiring-ground. After those for hire are disposed of, those for sale are called up.

O, you happy free women, contrast your New Year's day with that of the poor bond-woman! With you it is a pleasant season, and the light of the day is blessed. Friendly wishes meet you every where, and gifts are showered upon you. Even hearts that have been estranged from you soften at this season, and lips that have been silent echo back, "I wish you a happy New Year." Children bring their little offerings, and raise their rosy lips for a caress. They are your own, and no hand but that of death can take them from you.

But to the slave mother New Year's day comes laden with peculiar sorrows. She sits on her cold cabin floor, watching the children who may all be torn from her the next morning; and often does she wish that she and they might die before the day dawns. She may be an ignorant creature, degraded by the system that has brutalized her from childhood; but she has a mother's instincts, and is capable of feeling a mother's agonies.

On one of these sale days, I saw a mother lead seven children to the auction-block. She knew that some of them would be taken from her; but they took all. The children were sold to a slave-trader, and their mother was bought by a man in her own town. Before night her children were all far away. She begged the trader to tell her where he intended to take them; this he refused to do. How could he, when he knew he would sell them, one by one, wherever he could command the highest price? I met that mother in the street, and her wild, haggard face lives to-day in my mind. She wrung her hands in anguish, and exclaimed, "Gone! All gone! Why don't God kill me?" I had no words wherewith to comfort her. Instances of this kind are of daily, yea, of hourly occurrence.

Slaveholders have a method, peculiar to their institution, of getting rid of old slaves, whose lives have been worn out in their service. I knew an old woman, who for seventy years faithfully served her master. She had become almost helpless, from hard labor and disease. Her owners moved to Alabama, and the old black woman was left to be sold to any body who would give twenty dollars for her.

CHAPTER FOUR

The Slave Who Dared To Feel Like A Man.

Two years had passed since I entered Dr. Flint's family, and those years had brought much of the knowledge that comes from experience, though they had afforded little opportunity for any other kinds of knowledge.

My grandmother had, as much as possible, been a mother to her orphan grandchildren. By perseverance and unwearied industry, she was now mistress of a snug little home, surrounded with the necessaries of life. She would have been happy could her children have shared them with her. There remained but three children and two grandchildren, all slaves. Most earnestly did she strive to make us feel that it was the will of God: that He had seen fit to place us under such circumstances; and though it seemed hard, we ought to pray for contentment.

It was a beautiful faith, coming from a mother who could not call her children her own. But I, and Benjamin, her youngest boy, condemned it. We reasoned that it was much more the will of God that we should be situated as she was. We longed for a home like hers. There we always found sweet balsam for our troubles. She was so loving, so sympathizing! She always met us with a smile, and listened with patience to all our sorrows. She spoke so hopefully, that unconsciously the clouds gave place to sunshine. There was a grand big oven there, too, that baked bread and nice things for the town, and we knew there was always a choice bit in store for us.

But, alas! Even the charms of the old oven failed to reconcile us to our hard lot. Benjamin was now a tall, handsome lad, strongly and gracefully made, and with a spirit too bold and daring for a slave. My brother William, now twelve years old, had the same aversion to the word master that he had when he was an urchin of seven years. I was his confidant. He came to me with all his troubles. I remember one instance in particular. It was on a lovely spring morning, and when I marked the sunlight dancing here and there, its beauty seemed to mock my sadness. For my master, whose restless, craving, vicious nature roved about day and night, seeking whom to devour, had just left me, with stinging, scorching words; words that scathed ear and brain like fire. O, how I despised him! I thought how glad I should be, if some day when he walked the earth, it would open and swallow him up, and disencumber the world of a plague.

When he told me that I was made for his use, made to obey his command in every thing; that I was nothing but a slave, whose will must and should surrender to his, never before had my puny arm felt half so strong.

So deeply was I absorbed in painful reflections afterwards, that I neither saw nor heard the entrance of any one, till the voice of William sounded close beside me. "Linda," said he, "what makes you look so sad? I love you. O, Linda, isn't this a bad world? Every body seems so cross and unhappy. I wish I had died when poor father did."

I told him that every body was not cross, or unhappy; that those who had pleasant homes, and kind friends, and who were not afraid to love them, were happy. But we, who were slave-children, without father or mother, could not expect to be happy. We must be good; perhaps that would bring us contentment.

"Yes," he said, "I try to be good; but what's the use? They are all the time troubling me." Then he proceeded to relate his afternoon's difficulty with young master Nicholas. It seemed that the brother of master Nicholas had pleased himself with making up stories about William. Master Nicholas said he should be flogged, and he would do it. Whereupon he went to work; but William fought bravely, and the young master, finding he was getting the better of him, undertook to tie his hands behind him. He failed in that likewise. By dint of kicking and fisting, William came out of the skirmish none the worse for a few scratches.

He continued to discourse, on his young master's meanness; how he whipped the little boys, but was a perfect coward when a tussle ensued between him and white boys of his own size. On such occasions he always took to his legs. William had other charges to make against him. One was his rubbing up pennies with quicksilver, and passing them off for quarters of a dollar on an old man who kept a fruit stall. William was often sent to buy fruit, and he earnestly inquired of me what he ought to do under such circumstances. I told him it was certainly wrong to deceive the old man, and that it was his duty to tell him of the impositions practised by his young master. I assured him the old man would not be slow to comprehend the whole, and there the matter would end. William thought it might with the old man, but not with him. He said he did not mind the smart of the whip, but he did not like the idea of being whipped.

While I advised him to be good and forgiving I was not unconscious of the beam in my own eye. It was the very knowledge of my own shortcomings that urged me to retain, if possible, some sparks of my brother's God-given nature. I had not lived fourteen years in slavery for nothing. I had felt, seen, and heard enough, to read the characters, and question the motives, of those around me. The war of my life had begun; and though one of God's most powerless creatures, I resolved never to be conquered. Alas, for me!

If there was one pure, sunny spot for me, I believed it to be in Benjamin's heart, and in another's, whom I loved with all the ardor of a girl's first love. My owner knew of it, and sought in every way to render me miserable. He did not resort to corporal punishment, but to all the petty, tyrannical ways that human ingenuity could devise.

I remember the first time I was punished. It was in the month of February. My grandmother had taken my old shoes, and replaced them with a new pair. I needed them; for several inches of snow had fallen, and it still continued to fall. When I walked through Mrs. Flint's room, their creaking grated harshly on her refined nerves. She called me to her, and asked what I had about me that made such a horrid noise. I told her it was my new shoes. "Take them off," said she; "and if you put them on again, I'll throw them into the fire."

I took them off, and my stockings also. She then sent me a long distance, on an errand. As I went through the snow, my bare feet tingled. That night I was very hoarse; and I went to bed thinking the next day would find me sick, perhaps dead. What was my grief on waking to find myself quite well!

I had imagined if I died, or was laid up for some time, that my mistress would feel a twinge of remorse that she had so hated "the little imp," as she styled me. It was my ignorance of that mistress that gave rise to such extravagant imaginings.

Dr. Flint occasionally had high prices offered for me; but he always said, "She don't belong to me. She is my daughter's property, and I have no right to sell her." Good, honest man! My young mistress was still a child, and I could look for no protection from her. I loved her, and she returned my affection. I once heard her father allude to her attachment to me; and his wife promptly replied that it proceeded from fear. This put unpleasant doubts into my mind. Did the child feign what she did not feel? or was her mother jealous of the mite of love she bestowed on me? I concluded it must be the latter. I said to myself, "Surely, little children are true."

One afternoon I sat at my sewing, feeling unusual depression of spirits. My mistress had been accusing me of an offence, of which I assured her I was perfectly innocent; but I saw, by the contemptuous curl of her lip, that she believed I was telling a lie.

I wondered for what wise purpose God was leading me through such thorny paths, and whether still darker days were in store for me. As I sat musing thus, the door opened softly, and William came in. "Well, brother," said I, "what is the matter this time?"

"O Linda, Ben and his master have had a dreadful time!" said he.

My first thought was that Benjamin was killed. "Don't be frightened, Linda," said William; "I will tell you all about it."

It appeared that Benjamin's master had sent for him, and he did not immediately obey the summons. When he did, his master was angry, and began to whip him. He resisted. Master and slave fought, and finally the master was thrown. Benjamin had cause to tremble; for he had thrown to the ground his master—one of the richest men in town. I anxiously awaited the result.

That night I stole to my grandmother's house, and Benjamin also stole thither from his master's. My grandmother had gone to spend a day or two with an old friend living in the country.

"I have come," said Benjamin, "to tell you good by. I am going away."

I inquired where.

"To the north," he replied.

I looked at him to see whether he was in earnest. I saw it all in his firm, set mouth. I implored him not to go, but he paid no heed to my words. He said he was no longer a boy, and every day made his yoke more galling. He had raised his hand against his master, and was to be publicly whipped for the offence. I reminded him of the poverty and hardships he must encounter among strangers. I told him he might be caught and brought back; and that was terrible to think of.

He grew vexed, and asked if poverty and hardships with freedom, were not preferable to our treatment in slavery. "Linda," he continued, "we are dogs here; foot-balls, cattle, every thing that's mean. No, I will not stay. Let them bring me back. We don't die but once."

He was right; but it was hard to give him up. "Go," said I, "and break your mother's heart."

I repented of my words ere they were out.

"Linda," said he, speaking as I had not heard him speak that evening, "how could you say that? Poor mother! be kind to her, Linda; and you, too, cousin Fanny."

Cousin Fanny was a friend who had lived some years with us.

Farewells were exchanged, and the bright, kind boy, endeared to us by so many acts of love, vanished from our sight.

It is not necessary to state how he made his escape. Suffice it to say, he was on his way to New York when a violent storm overtook the vessel. The captain said he must put into the nearest port. This alarmed Benjamin, who was aware that he would be advertised in every port near his own town. His embarrassment was noticed by the captain. To port they went. There the advertisement met the captain's eye. Benjamin so exactly answered its description, that the captain laid hold on him, and bound him in chains. The storm passed, and they proceeded to New York. Before reaching that port Benjamin managed to get off his chains and throw them overboard. He escaped from the vessel, but was pursued, captured, and carried back to his master.

When my grandmother returned home and found her youngest child had fled, great was her sorrow; but, with characteristic piety, she said, "God's will be done." Each morning, she inquired if any news had been heard from her boy. Yes, news was heard. The master was rejoicing over a letter, announcing the capture of his human chattel.

That day seems but as yesterday, so well do I remember it. I saw him led through the streets in chains, to jail. His face was ghastly pale, yet full of determination. He had begged one of the sailors to go to his mother's house and ask her not to meet him. He said the sight of her distress would take from him all self-control. She yearned to see him, and she went; but she screened herself in the crowd, that it might be as her child had said.

We were not allowed to visit him; but we had known the jailer for years, and he was a kind-hearted man. At midnight he opened the jail door for my grandmother and myself to enter, in disguise. When we entered the cell not a sound broke the stillness. "Benjamin, Benjamin!" whispered my grandmother. No answer. "Benjamin!" she again faltered. There was a jingle of chains. The moon had just risen, and cast an uncertain light through the bars of the window. We knelt down and took Benjamin's cold hands in ours. We did not speak. Sobs were heard, and Benjamin's lips were unsealed; for his mother was weeping on his neck. How vividly does memory bring back that sad night! Mother and son talked together. He asked her pardon for the suffering he had caused her. She said she had nothing to forgive; she could not blame his desire for freedom. He told her that when he was captured, he broke away, and was about casting himself into the river, when thoughts of her came over him, and he desisted. She asked if he did not also think of God. I fancied I saw his face grow fierce in the moonlight. He answered, "No, I did not think of him. When a man is hunted like a wild beast he forgets there is a God, a heaven. He forgets every thing in his struggle to get beyond the reach of the bloodhounds."

"Don't talk so, Benjamin," said she. "Put your trust in God. Be humble, my child, and your master will forgive you."

"Forgive me for what, mother? For not letting him treat me like a dog? No! I will never humble myself to him. I have worked for him for nothing all my life, and I am repaid with stripes and imprisonment. Here I will stay till I die, or till he sells me."

The poor mother shuddered at his words. I think he felt it; for when he next spoke, his voice was calmer. "Don't fret about me, mother. I ain't worth it," said he. "I wish I had some of your goodness. You bear every thing patiently, just as though you thought it was all right. I wish I could."

She told him she had not always been so; once, she was like him; but when sore troubles came upon her, and she had no arm to lean upon, she learned to call on God, and he lightened her burdens. She besought him to do likewise.

We overstaid our time, and were obliged to hurry from the jail.

Benjamin had been imprisoned three weeks, when my grandmother went to intercede for him with his master. He was immovable. He said Benjamin should serve as an example to the rest of his slaves; he should be kept in jail till he was subdued, or be sold if he got but one dollar for him. However, he afterwards relented in some degree. The chains were taken off, and we were allowed to visit him.

As his food was of the coarsest kind, we carried him as often as possible a warm supper, accompanied with some little luxury for the jailer.

Three months elapsed, and there was no prospect of release or of a purchaser. One day he was heard to sing and laugh. This piece of indecorum was told to his master, and the overseer was ordered to re-chain him. He was now confined in an apartment with other prisoners, who were covered with filthy rags. Benjamin was chained near them, and was soon covered with vermin. He worked at his chains till he succeeded in getting out of them. He passed them through the bars of the window, with a request that they should be taken to his master, and he should be informed that he was covered with vermin.

This audacity was punished with heavier chains, and prohibition of our visits.

My grandmother continued to send him fresh changes of clothes. The old ones were burned up. The last night we saw him in jail his mother still begged him to send for his master, and beg his pardon. Neither persuasion nor argument could turn him from his purpose. He calmly answered, "I am waiting his time."

Those chains were mournful to hear.

Another three months passed, and Benjamin left his prison walls. We that loved him waited to bid him a long and last farewell. A slave trader had bought him. You remember, I told you what price he brought when ten years of age. Now he was more than twenty years old, and sold for three hundred dollars. The master had been blind to his own interest. Long confinement had made his face too pale, his form too thin; moreover, the trader had heard something of his character, and it did not strike him as suitable for a slave. He said he would give any price if the handsome lad was a girl. We thanked God that he was not.

Could you have seen that mother clinging to her child, when they fastened the irons upon his wrists; could you have heard her heart-rending groans, and seen her bloodshot eyes wander wildly from face to face, vainly pleading for mercy; could you have witnessed that scene as I saw it, you would exclaim, Slavery is damnable!

Benjamin, her youngest, her pet, was forever gone! She could not realize it. She had had an interview with the trader for the purpose of ascertaining if Benjamin could be purchased. She was told it was impossible, as he had given bonds not to sell him till he was out of the state. He promised that he would not sell him till he reached New Orleans.

With a strong arm and unvaried trust, my grandmother began her work of love. Benjamin must be free. If she succeeded, she knew they would still be separated; but the sacrifice was not too great. Day and night she labored. The trader's price would treble that he gave; but she was not discouraged.

She employed a lawyer to write to a gentleman, whom she knew, in New Orleans. She begged him to interest himself for Benjamin, and he willingly favored her request. When he saw Benjamin, and stated his business, he thanked him; but said he preferred to wait a while before making the trader an offer. He knew he had tried to obtain a high price for him, and had invariably failed. This encouraged him to make another effort for freedom. So one morning, long before day, Benjamin was missing. He was riding over the blue billows, bound for Baltimore.

For once his white face did him a kindly service. They had no suspicion that it belonged to a slave; otherwise, the law would have been followed out to the letter, and the thing rendered back to slavery. The brightest skies are often overshadowed by the darkest clouds. Benjamin was taken sick, and compelled to remain in Baltimore three weeks. His strength was slow in returning; and his desire to continue his journey seemed to retard his recovery. How could he get strength without air and exercise? He resolved to venture on a short walk. A by-street was selected, where he thought himself secure of not being met by any one that knew him; but a voice called out, "Halloo, Ben, my boy! what are you doing here?"

His first impulse was to run; but his legs trembled so that he could not stir. He turned to confront his antagonist, and behold, there stood his old master's next door neighbor! He thought it was all over with him now; but it proved otherwise. That man was a miracle. He possessed a goodly number of slaves, and yet was not quite deaf to that mystic clock, whose ticking is rarely heard in the slaveholder's breast.

"Ben, you are sick," said he. "Why, you look like a ghost. I guess I gave you something of a start. Never mind, Ben, I am not going to touch you. You had a pretty tough time of it, and you may go on your way rejoicing for all me. But I would advise you to get out of this place plaguy quick, for there are several gentlemen here from our town." He described the nearest and safest route to New York, and added, "I shall be glad to tell your mother I have seen you. Good by, Ben."

Benjamin turned away, filled with gratitude, and surprised that the town he hated contained such a gem—a gem worthy of a purer setting.

This gentleman was a Northerner by birth, and had married a southern lady. On his return, he told my grandmother that he had seen her son, and of the service he had rendered him.

Benjamin reached New York safely, and concluded to stop there until he had gained strength enough to proceed further. It happened that my grandmother's only remaining son had sailed for the same city on business for his mistress. Through God's providence, the brothers met. You may be sure it was a happy meeting. "O Phil," exclaimed Benjamin, "I am here at last." Then he told him how near he came to dying, almost in sight of free land, and how he prayed that he might live to get one breath of free air. He said life was worth something now, and it would be hard to die. In the old jail he had not valued it; once, he was tempted to destroy it; but something, he did not know what, had prevented him; perhaps it was fear. He had heard those who profess to be religious declare there was no heaven for self-murderers; and as his life had been pretty hot here, he did not desire a continuation of the same in another world. "If I die now," he exclaimed, "thank God, I shall die a freeman!"

He begged my uncle Phillip not to return south; but stay and work with him, till they earned enough to buy those at home. His brother told him it would kill their mother if he deserted her in her trouble. She had pledged her house, and with difficulty had raised money to buy him. Would he be bought?

"No, never!" he replied. "Do you suppose, Phil, when I have got so far out of their clutches, I will give them one red cent? No! And do you suppose I would turn mother out of her home in her old age? That I would let her pay all those hard-earned dollars for me, and never to see me? For you know she will stay south as long as her other children are slaves. What a good mother! Tell her to buy you, Phil. You have been a comfort to her, and I have been a trouble. And Linda, poor Linda; what'll become of her? Phil, you don't know what a life they lead her. She has told me something about it, and I wish old Flint was dead, or a better man. When I was in jail, he asked her if she didn't want him to ask my master to forgive me, and take me home again. She told him, No; that I didn't want to go back. He got mad, and said we were all alike. I never despised my own master half as much as I do that man. There is many a worse slaveholder than my master; but for all that I would not be his slave."

While Benjamin was sick, he had parted with nearly all his clothes to pay necessary expenses. But he did not part with a little pin I fastened in his bosom when we parted. It was the most valuable thing I owned, and I thought none more worthy to wear it. He had it still.

His brother furnished him with clothes, and gave him what money he had.

They parted with moistened eyes; and as Benjamin turned away, he said, "Phil, I part with all my kindred." And so it proved. We never heard from him again.

Uncle Phillip came home; and the first words he uttered when he entered the house were, "Mother, Ben is free! I have seen him in New York." She stood looking at him with a bewildered air. "Mother, don't you believe it?" he said, laying his hand softly upon her shoulder. She raised her hands, and exclaimed, "God be praised! Let us thank him." She dropped on her knees, and poured forth her heart in prayer. Then Phillip must sit down and repeat to her every word Benjamin had said. He told her all; only he forbore to mention how sick and pale her darling looked. Why should he distress her when she could do him no good?

The brave old woman still toiled on, hoping to rescue some of her other children. After a while she succeeded in buying Phillip. She paid eight hundred dollars, and came home with the precious document that secured his freedom. The happy mother and son sat together by the old hearthstone that night, telling how proud they were of each other, and how they would prove to the world that they could take care of themselves, as they had long taken care of others. We all concluded by saying, "He that is willing to be a slave, let him be a slave."

CHAPTER FIVE

The Trials Of Girlhood.

During the first years of my service in Dr. Flint's family, I was accustomed to share some indulgences with the children of my mistress. Though this seemed to me no more than right, I was grateful for it, and tried to merit the kindness by the faithful discharge of my duties. But I now entered on my fifteenth year—a sad epoch in the life of a slave girl. My master began to whisper foul words in my ear. Young as I was, I could not remain ignorant of their import. I tried to treat them with indifference or contempt. The master's age, my extreme youth, and the fear that his conduct would be reported to my grandmother, made him bear this treatment for many months. He was a crafty man, and resorted to many means to accomplish his purposes. Sometimes he had stormy, terrific ways, that made his victims tremble; sometimes he assumed a gentleness that he thought must surely subdue. Of the two, I preferred his stormy moods, although they left me trembling. He tried his utmost to corrupt the pure principles my grandmother had instilled. He peopled my young mind with unclean images, such as only a vile monster could think of. I turned from him with disgust and hatred. But he was my master. I was compelled to live under the same roof with him—where I saw a man forty years my senior daily violating the most sacred commandments of nature. He told me I was his property; that I must be subject to his will in all things. My soul revolted against the mean tyranny. But where could I turn for protection? No matter whether the slave girl be as black as ebony or as fair as her mistress. In either case, there is no shadow of law to protect her from insult, from violence, or even from death; all these are inflicted by fiends who bear the shape of men. The mistress, who ought to protect the helpless victim, has no other feelings towards her but those of jealousy and rage. The degradation, the wrongs, the vices, that grow out of slavery, are more than I can describe. They are greater than you would willingly believe. Surely, if you credited one half the truths that are told you concerning the helpless millions suffering in this cruel bondage, you at the north would not help to tighten the yoke. You surely would refuse to do for the master, on your own soil, the mean and cruel work which trained bloodhounds and the lowest class of whites do for him at the south.

Every where the years bring to all enough of sin and sorrow; but in slavery the very dawn of life is darkened by these shadows. Even the little child, who is accustomed to wait on her mistress and her children, will learn, before she is twelve years old, why it is that her mistress hates such and such a one among the slaves. Perhaps the child's own mother is among those hated ones. She listens to violent outbreaks of jealous passion, and cannot help understanding what is the cause. She will become prematurely knowing in evil things. Soon she will learn to tremble when she hears her master's footfall. She will be compelled to realize that she is no longer a child. If God has bestowed beauty upon her, it will prove her greatest curse. That which commands admiration in the white woman only hastens the degradation of the female slave. I know that some are too much brutalized by slavery to feel the humiliation of their position; but many slaves feel it most acutely, and shrink from the memory of it. I cannot tell how much I suffered in the presence of these wrongs, nor how I am still pained by the retrospect. My master met me at every turn, reminding me that I belonged to him, and swearing by heaven and earth that he would compel me to submit to him. If I went out for a breath of fresh air, after a day of unwearied toil, his footsteps dogged me. If I knelt by my mother's grave, his dark shadow fell on me even there. The light heart which nature had given me became heavy with sad forebodings. The other slaves in my master's house noticed the change. Many of them pitied me; but none dared to ask the cause. They had no need to inquire. They knew too well the guilty practices under that roof; and they were aware that to speak of them was an offence that never went unpunished.

I longed for some one to confide in. I would have given the world to have laid my head on my grandmother's faithful bosom, and told her all my troubles. But Dr. Flint swore he would kill me, if I was not as silent as the grave. Then, although my grandmother was all in all to me, I feared her as well as loved her. I had been accustomed to look up to her with a respect bordering upon awe. I was very young, and felt shamefaced about telling her such impure things, especially as I knew her to be very strict on such subjects. Moreover, she was a woman of a high spirit. She was usually very quiet in her demeanor; but if her indignation was once roused, it was not very easily quelled. I had been told that she once chased a white gentleman with a loaded pistol, because he insulted one of her daughters. I dreaded the consequences of a violent outbreak; and both pride and fear kept me silent. But though I did not confide in my grandmother, and even evaded her vigilant watchfulness and inquiry, her presence in the neighborhood was some protection to me. Though she had been a slave, Dr. Flint was afraid of her. He dreaded her scorching rebukes. Moreover, she was known and patronized by many people; and he did not wish to have his villany made public. It was lucky for me that I did not live on a distant plantation, but in a town not so large that the inhabitants were ignorant of each other's affairs. Bad as are the laws and customs in a slaveholding community, the doctor, as a professional man, deemed it prudent to keep up some outward show of decency.

O, what days and nights of fear and sorrow that man caused me! Reader, it is not to awaken sympathy for myself that I am telling you truthfully what I suffered in slavery. I do it to kindle a flame of compassion in your hearts for my sisters who are still in bondage, suffering as I once suffered.

I once saw two beautiful children playing together. One was a fair white child; the other was her slave, and also her sister. When I saw them embracing each other, and heard their joyous laughter, I turned sadly away from the lovely sight. I foresaw the inevitable blight that would fall on the little slave's heart. I knew how soon her laughter would be changed to sighs. The fair child grew up to be a still fairer woman. From childhood to womanhood her pathway was blooming with flowers, and overarched by a sunny sky. Scarcely one day of her life had been clouded when the sun rose on her happy bridal morning.

How had those years dealt with her slave sister, the little playmate of her childhood? She, also, was very beautiful; but the flowers and sunshine of love were not for her. She drank the cup of sin, and shame, and misery, whereof her persecuted race are compelled to drink.

In view of these things, why are ye silent, ye free men and women of the north? Why do your tongues falter in maintenance of the right? Would that I had more ability! But my heart is so full, and my pen is so weak! There are noble men and women who plead for us, striving to help those who cannot help themselves. God bless them! God give them strength and courage to go on! God bless those, every where, who are laboring to advance the cause of humanity!

The Jealous Mistress.

I would ten thousand times rather that my children should be the half-starved paupers of Ireland than to be the most pampered among the slaves of America. I would rather drudge out my life on a cotton plantation, till the grave opened to give me rest, than to live with an unprincipled master and a jealous mistress. The felon's home in a penitentiary is preferable. He may repent, and turn from the error of his ways, and so find peace; but it is not so with a favorite slave. She is not allowed to have any pride of character. It is deemed a crime in her to wish to be virtuous.

Mrs. Flint possessed the key to her husband's character before I was born. She might have used this knowledge to counsel and to screen the young and the innocent among her slaves; but for them she had no sympathy. They were the objects of her constant suspicion and malevolence. She watched her husband with unceasing vigilance; but he was well practised in means to evade it. What he could not find opportunity to say in words he manifested in signs. He invented more than were ever thought of in a deaf and dumb asylum. I let them pass, as if I did not understand what he meant; and many were the curses and threats bestowed on me for my stupidity. One day he caught me teaching myself to write. He frowned, as if he was not well pleased; but I suppose he came to the conclusion that such an accomplishment might help to advance his favorite scheme. Before long, notes were often slipped into my hand. I would return them, saying, "I can't read them, sir." "Can't you?" he replied; "then I must read them to you." He always finished the reading by asking, "Do you understand?" Sometimes he would complain of the heat of the tea room, and order his supper to be placed on a small table in the piazza. He would seat himself there with a well-satisfied smile, and tell me to stand by and brush away the flies. He would eat very slowly, pausing between the mouthfuls. These intervals were employed in describing the happiness I was so foolishly throwing away, and in threatening me with the penalty that finally awaited my stubborn disobedience. He boasted much of the forbearance he had exercised towards me, and reminded me that there was a limit to his patience. When I succeeded in avoiding opportunities for him to talk to me at home, I was ordered to come to his office, to do some errand. When there, I was obliged to stand and listen to such language as he saw fit to address to me. Sometimes I so openly expressed my contempt for him that he would become violently enraged, and I wondered why he did not strike me. Circumstanced as he was, he probably thought it was better policy to be forbearing. But the state of things grew worse and worse daily. In desperation I told him that I must and would apply to my grandmother for protection. He threatened me with death, and worse than death, if I made any complaint to her. Strange to say, I did not despair. I was naturally of a buoyant disposition, and always I had a hope of somehow getting out of his clutches. Like many a poor, simple slave before me, I trusted that some threads of joy would yet be woven into my dark destiny.

I had entered my sixteenth year, and every day it became more apparent that my presence was intolerable to Mrs. Flint. Angry words frequently passed between her and her husband. He had never punished me himself, and he would not allow any body else to punish me. In that respect, she was never satisfied; but, in her angry moods, no terms were too vile for her to bestow upon me. Yet I, whom she detested so bitterly, had far more pity for her than he had, whose duty it was to make her life happy. I never wronged her, or wished to wrong her; and one word of kindness from her would have brought me to her feet.

After repeated quarrels between the doctor and his wife, he announced his intention to take his youngest daughter, then four years old, to sleep in his apartment. It was necessary that a servant should sleep in the same room, to be on hand if the child stirred. I was selected for that office, and informed for what purpose that arrangement had been made. By managing to keep within sight of people, as much as possible, during the day time, I had hitherto succeeded in eluding my master, though a razor was often held to my throat to force me to change this line of policy. At night I slept by the side of my great aunt, where I felt safe. He was too prudent to come into her room. She was an old woman, and had been in the family many years. Moreover, as a married man, and a professional man, he deemed it necessary to save appearances in some degree. But he resolved to remove the obstacle in the way of his scheme; and he thought he had planned it so that he should evade suspicion. He was well aware how much I prized my refuge by the side of my old aunt, and he determined to dispossess me of it. The first night the doctor had the little child in his room alone. The next morning, I was ordered to take my station as nurse the following night. A kind

Providence interposed in my favor. During the day Mrs. Flint heard of this new arrangement, and a storm followed. I rejoiced to hear it rage.

After a while my mistress sent for me to come to her room. Her first question was, "Did you know you were to sleep in the doctor's room?"

"Yes, ma'am."

"Who told you?"

"My master."

"Will you answer truly all the questions I ask?"

"Yes, ma'am."

"Tell me, then, as you hope to be forgiven, are you innocent of what I have accused you?"

"I am."

She handed me a Bible, and said, "Lay your hand on your heart, kiss this holy book, and swear before God that you tell me the truth."

I took the oath she required, and I did it with a clear conscience.

"You have taken God's holy word to testify your innocence," said she. "If you have deceived me, beware! Now take this stool, sit down, look me directly in the face, and tell me all that has passed between your master and you."

I did as she ordered. As I went on with my account her color changed frequently, she wept, and sometimes groaned. She spoke in tones so sad, that I was touched by her grief. The tears came to my eyes; but I was soon convinced that her emotions arose from anger and wounded pride. She felt that her marriage vows were desecrated, her dignity insulted; but she had no compassion for the poor victim of her husband's perfidy. She pitied herself as a martyr; but she was incapable of feeling for the condition of shame and misery in which her unfortunate, helpless slave was placed.

Yet perhaps she had some touch of feeling for me; for when the conference was ended, she spoke kindly, and promised to protect me. I should have been much comforted by this assurance if I could have had confidence in it; but my experiences in slavery had filled me with distrust. She was not a very refined woman, and had not much control over her passions. I was an object of her jealousy, and, consequently, of her hatred; and I knew I could not expect kindness or confidence from her under the circumstances in which I was placed. I could not blame her. Slaveholders' wives feel as other women would under similar circumstances. The fire of her temper kindled from small sparks, and now the flame became so intense that the doctor was obliged to give up his intended arrangement.

I knew I had ignited the torch, and I expected to suffer for it afterwards; but I felt too thankful to my mistress for the timely aid she rendered me to care much about that. She now took me to sleep in a room adjoining her own. There I was an object of her especial care, though not of her especial comfort, for she spent many a sleepless night to watch over me. Sometimes I woke up, and found her bending over me. At other times she whispered in my ear, as though it was her husband who was speaking to me, and listened to hear what I would answer. If she startled me, on such occasions, she would glide stealthily away; and the next morning she would tell me I had been talking in my sleep, and ask who I was talking to. At last, I began to be fearful for my life. It had been often threatened; and you can imagine, better than I can describe, what an unpleasant sensation it must produce to wake up in the dead of night and find a jealous woman bending over you. Terrible as this experience was, I had fears that it would give place to one more terrible.

My mistress grew weary of her vigils; they did not prove satisfactory. She changed her tactics. She now tried the trick of accusing my master of crime, in my presence, and gave my name as the author of the accusation. To my utter astonishment, he replied, "I don't believe it; but if she did acknowledge it, you tortured her into exposing me." Tortured into exposing him! Truly, Satan had no difficulty in distinguishing the color of his soul! I understood his object in making this false representation. It was to show me that I gained nothing by seeking the protection of my mistress; that the power was still all in his own hands. I pitied Mrs. Flint. She was a second wife, many years the junior of her husband; and the hoary-headed miscreant was enough to try the patience of a wiser and better woman. She was completely foiled, and knew not how to proceed. She would gladly have had me flogged for my supposed false oath; but, as I have already stated, the doctor never allowed any one to whip me. The old sinner was politic. The application of the lash might have led to remarks that would have exposed him in the eyes of his children and grandchildren. How often did I rejoice that I lived in a town where all the inhabitants knew each other! If I had been on a remote plantation, or lost among the multitude of a crowded city, I should not be a living woman at this day.

The secrets of slavery are concealed like those of the Inquisition. My master was, to my knowledge, the father of eleven slaves. But did the mothers dare to tell who was the father of their children? Did the other slaves dare to allude to it, except in whispers among themselves? No, indeed! They knew too well the terrible consequences.

My grandmother could not avoid seeing things which excited her suspicions. She was uneasy about me, and tried various ways to buy me; but the never-changing answer was always repeated: "Linda does not belong to me. She is my daughter's property, and I have no legal right to sell her." The conscientious man! He was too scrupulous to sell me; but he had no scruples whatever about committing a much greater wrong against the helpless young girl placed under his guardianship, as his daughter's property. Sometimes my persecutor would ask me whether I would like to be sold. I told him I would rather be sold to any body than to lead such a life as I did. On such occasions he would assume the air of a very injured individual, and reproach me for my ingratitude. "Did I not take you into the house, and make you the companion of my own children?" he would say. "Have I ever treated you like a negro? I have never allowed you to be punished, not even to please your mistress. And this is the recompense I get, you ungrateful girl!" I answered that he had reasons of his own for screening me from punishment, and that the course he pursued made my mistress hate me and persecute me. If I wept, he would say, "Poor child! Don't cry! don't cry! I will make peace for you with your mistress. Only let me arrange matters in my own way. Poor, foolish girl! you don't know what is for your own good. I would cherish you. I would make a lady of you. Now go, and think of all I have promised you."

I did think of it.

Reader, I draw no imaginary pictures of southern homes. I am telling you the plain truth. Yet when victims make their escape from this wild beast of Slavery, northerners consent to act the part of bloodhounds, and hunt the poor fugitive back into his den, "full of dead men's bones, and all uncleanness." Nay, more, they are not only willing, but proud, to give their daughters in marriage to slaveholders. The poor girls have romantic notions of a sunny clime, and of the flowering vines that all the year round shade a happy home. To what disappointments are they destined! The young wife soon learns that the husband in whose hands she has placed her happiness pays no regard to his marriage vows. Children of every shade of complexion play with her own fair babies, and too well she knows that they are born unto him of his own household. Jealousy and hatred enter the flowery home, and it is ravaged of its loveliness.

Southern women often marry a man knowing that he is the father of many little slaves. They do not trouble themselves about it. They regard such children as property, as marketable as the pigs on the plantation; and it is seldom that they do not make them aware of this by passing them into the slave-trader's hands as soon as possible, and thus getting them out of their sight. I am glad to say there are some honorable exceptions.

I have myself known two southern wives who exhorted their husbands to free those slaves towards whom they stood in a "parental relation;" and their request was granted. These husbands blushed before the superior nobleness of their wives' natures. Though they had only counselled them to do that which it was their duty to do, it commanded their respect, and rendered their conduct more exemplary. Concealment was at an end, and confidence took the place of distrust.

Though this bad institution deadens the moral sense, even in white women, to a fearful extent, it is not altogether extinct. I have heard southern ladies say of Mr. Such a one, "He not only thinks it no disgrace to be the father of those little niggers, but he is not ashamed to call himself their master. I declare, such things ought not to be tolerated in any decent society!"

The Lover

Why does the slave ever love? Why allow the tendrils of the heart to twine around objects which may at any moment be wrenched away by the hand of violence? When separations come by the hand of death, the pious soul can bow in resignation, and say, "Not my will, but thine be done, O Lord!" But when the ruthless hand of man strikes the blow, regardless of the misery he causes, it is hard to be submissive. I did not reason thus when I was a young girl. Youth will be youth. I loved, and I indulged the hope that the dark clouds around me would turn out a bright lining. I forgot that in the land of my birth the shadows are too dense for light to penetrate. A land

"Where laughter is not mirth; nor thought the mind;
Nor words a language; nor e'en men mankind.
Where cries reply to curses, shrieks to blows,
And each is tortured in his separate hell."

There was in the neighborhood a young colored carpenter; a free-born man. We had been well acquainted in childhood, and frequently met together afterwards. We became mutually attached, and he proposed to marry me. I loved him with all the ardor of a young girl's first love. But when I reflected that I was a slave, and that the laws gave no sanction to the marriage of such, my heart sank within me. My lover wanted to buy me; but I knew that Dr. Flint was too wilful and arbitrary a man to consent to that arrangement. From him, I was sure of experiencing all sorts of opposition, and I had nothing to hope from my mistress. She would have been delighted to have got rid of me, but not in that way. It would have relieved her mind of a burden if she could have seen me sold to some distant state, but if I was married near home I should be just as much in her husband's power as I had previously been,—for the husband of a slave has no power to protect her. Moreover, my mistress, like many others, seemed to think that slaves had no right to any family ties of their own; that they were created merely to wait upon the family of the mistress. I once heard her abuse a young slave girl, who told her that a colored man wanted to make her his wife. "I will have you peeled and pickled, my lady," said she, "if I ever hear you mention that subject again. Do you suppose that I will have you tending my children with the children of that nigger?" The girl to whom she said this had a mulatto child, of course not acknowledged by its father. The poor black man who loved her would have been proud to acknowledge his helpless offspring.

Many and anxious were the thoughts I revolved in my mind. I was at a loss what to do. Above all things, I was desirous to spare my lover the insults that had cut so deeply into my own soul. I talked with my grandmother about it, and partly told her my fears. I did not dare to tell her the worst. She had long suspected all was not right, and if I confirmed her suspicions I knew a storm would rise that would prove the overthrow of all my hopes.

This love-dream had been my support through many trials; and I could not bear to run the risk of having it suddenly dissipated. There was a lady in the neighborhood, a particular friend of Dr. Flint's, who often visited the house. I had a great respect for her, and she had always manifested a friendly interest in me. Grandmother thought she would have great influence with the doctor. I went to this lady, and told her my story. I told her I was aware that my lover's being a free-born man would prove a great objection; but he wanted to buy me; and if Dr. Flint would consent to that arrangement, I felt sure he would be willing to pay any reasonable price. She knew that Mrs. Flint disliked me; therefore, I ventured to suggest that perhaps my mistress would approve of my being sold, as that would rid her of me. The lady listened with kindly sympathy, and promised to do her utmost to promote my wishes. She had an interview with the doctor, and I believe she pleaded my cause earnestly; but it was all to no purpose.

How I dreaded my master now! Every minute I expected to be summoned to his presence; but the day passed, and I heard nothing from him. The next morning, a message was brought to me: "Master wants you in his study." I found the door ajar, and I stood a moment gazing at the hateful man who claimed a right to rule me, body and soul. I entered, and tried to appear calm. I did not want him to know how my heart was bleeding. He looked fixedly at me, with an expression which seemed to say, "I have half a mind to kill you on the spot." At last he broke the silence, and that was a relief to both of us.

"So you want to be married, do you?" said he, "and to a free nigger."

"Yes, sir."

"Well, I'll soon convince you whether I am your master, or the nigger fellow you honor so highly. If you must have a husband, you may take up with one of my slaves."

What a situation I should be in, as the wife of one of his slaves, even if my heart had been interested!

I replied, "Don't you suppose, sir, that a slave can have some preference about marrying? Do you suppose that all men are alike to her?"

"Do you love this nigger?" said he, abruptly.

"Yes, sir."

"How dare you tell me so!" he exclaimed, in great wrath. After a slight pause, he added, "I supposed you thought more of yourself; that you felt above the insults of such puppies."

I replied, "If he is a puppy I am a puppy, for we are both of the negro race. It is right and honorable for us to love each other. The man you call a puppy never insulted me, sir; and he would not love me if he did not believe me to be a virtuous woman."

He sprang upon me like a tiger, and gave me a stunning blow. It was the first time he had ever struck me; and fear did not enable me to control my anger. When I had recovered a little from the effects, I exclaimed, "You have struck me for answering you honestly. How I despise you!"

There was silence for some minutes. Perhaps he was deciding what should be my punishment; or, perhaps, he wanted to give me time to reflect on what I had said, and to whom I had said it. Finally, he asked, "Do you know what you have said?"

"Yes, sir; but your treatment drove me to it."

"Do you know that I have a right to do as I like with you,—that I can kill you, if I please?"

"You have tried to kill me, and I wish you had; but you have no right to do as you like with me."

"Silence!" he exclaimed, in a thundering voice. "By heavens, girl, you forget yourself too far! Are you mad?

If you are, I will soon bring you to your senses. Do you think any other master would bear what I have borne from you this morning? Many masters would have killed you on the spot. How would you like to be sent to jail for your insolence?”

“I know I have been disrespectful, sir,” I replied; “but you drove me to it; I couldn’t help it. As for the jail, there would be more peace for me there than there is here.”

“You deserve to go there,” said he, “and to be under such treatment, that you would forget the meaning of the word peace. It would do you good. It would take some of your high notions out of you. But I am not ready to send you there yet, notwithstanding your ingratitude for all my kindness and forbearance. You have been the plague of my life. I have wanted to make you happy, and I have been repaid with the basest ingratitude; but though you have proved yourself incapable of appreciating my kindness, I will be lenient towards you, Linda. I will give you one more chance to redeem your character. If you behave yourself and do as I require, I will forgive you and treat you as I always have done; but if you disobey me, I will punish you as I would the meanest slave on my plantation. Never let me hear that fellow’s name mentioned again. If I ever know of your speaking to him, I will cowhide you both; and if I catch him lurking about my premises, I will shoot him as soon as I would a dog. Do you hear what I say? I’ll teach you a lesson about marriage and free niggers! Now go, and let this be the last time I have occasion to speak to you on this subject.”

Reader, did you ever hate? I hope not. I never did but once; and I trust I never shall again. Somebody has called it “the atmosphere of hell;” and I believe it is so.

For a fortnight the doctor did not speak to me. He thought to mortify me; to make me feel that I had disgraced myself by receiving the honorable addresses of a respectable colored man, in preference to the base proposals of a white man. But though his lips disdained to address me, his eyes were very loquacious. No animal ever watched its prey more narrowly than he watched me. He knew that I could write, though he had failed to make me read his letters; and he was now troubled lest I should exchange letters with another man. After a while he became weary of silence; and I was sorry for it. One morning, as he passed through the hall, to leave the house, he contrived to thrust a note into my hand. I thought I had better read it, and spare myself the vexation of having him read it to me. It expressed regret for the blow he had given me, and reminded me that I myself was wholly to blame for it. He hoped I had become convinced of the injury I was doing myself by incurring his displeasure. He wrote that he had made up his mind to go to Louisiana; that he should take several slaves with him, and intended I should be one of the number. My mistress would remain where she was; therefore I should have nothing to fear from that quarter. If I merited kindness from him, he assured me that it would be lavishly bestowed. He begged me to think over the matter, and answer the following day.

The next morning I was called to carry a pair of scissors to his room. I laid them on the table, with the letter beside them. He thought it was my answer, and did not call me back. I went as usual to attend my young mistress to and from school. He met me in the street, and ordered me to stop at his office on my way back. When I entered, he showed me his letter, and asked me why I had not answered it. I replied, "I am your daughter's property, and it is in your power to send me, or take me, wherever you please." He said he was very glad to find me so willing to go, and that we should start early in the autumn. He had a large practice in the town, and I rather thought he had made up the story merely to frighten me. However that might be, I was determined that I would never go to Louisiana with him.

Summer passed away, and early in the autumn Dr. Flint's eldest son was sent to Louisiana to examine the country, with a view to emigrating. That news did not disturb me. I knew very well that I should not be sent with him. That I had not been taken to the plantation before this time, was owing to the fact that his son was there. He was jealous of his son; and jealousy of the overseer had kept him from punishing me by sending me into the fields to work. Is it strange that I was not proud of these protectors? As for the overseer, he was a man for whom I had less respect than I had for a bloodhound.

Young Mr. Flint did not bring back a favorable report of Louisiana, and I heard no more of that scheme. Soon after this, my lover met me at the corner of the street, and I stopped to speak to him. Looking up, I saw my master watching us from his window. I hurried home, trembling with fear. I was sent for, immediately, to go to his room. He met me with a blow. "When is mistress to be married?" said he, in a sneering tone. A shower of oaths and imprecations followed. How thankful I was that my lover was a free man! that my tyrant had no power to flog him for speaking to me in the street!

Again and again I revolved in my mind how all this would end. There was no hope that the doctor would consent to sell me on any terms. He had an iron will, and was determined to keep me, and to conquer me. My lover was an intelligent and religious man. Even if he could have obtained permission to marry me while I was a slave, the marriage would give him no power to protect me from my master. It would have made him miserable to witness the insults I should have been subjected to. And then, if we had children, I knew they must "follow the condition of the mother." What a terrible blight that would be on the heart of a free, intelligent father! For his sake, I felt that I ought not to link his fate with my own unhappy destiny. He was going to Savannah to see about a little property left him by an uncle; and hard as it was to bring my feelings to it, I earnestly entreated him not to come back. I advised him to go to the Free States, where his tongue would not be tied, and where his intelligence would be of more avail to him. He left me, still hoping the day would come when I could be bought. With me the lamp of hope had gone out. The dream of my girlhood was over. I felt lonely and desolate.

Still I was not stripped of all. I still had my good grandmother, and my affectionate brother. When he put his arms round my neck, and looked into my eyes, as if to read there the troubles I dared not tell, I felt that I still had something to love. But even that pleasant emotion was chilled by the reflection that he might be torn from me at any moment, by some sudden freak of my master. If he had known how we loved each other, I think he would have exulted in separating us. We often planned together how we could get to the north. But, as William remarked, such things are easier said than done. My movements were very closely watched, and we had no means of getting any money to defray our expenses. As for grandmother, she was strongly opposed to her children's undertaking any such project. She had not forgotten poor Benjamin's sufferings, and she was afraid that if another child tried to escape, he would have a similar or a worse fate. To me, nothing seemed more dreadful than my present life. I said to myself, "William must be free. He shall go to the north, and I will follow him." Many a slave sister has formed the same plans.

CHAPTER EIGHT

What Slaves Are Taught To Think Of The North.

Slaveholders pride themselves upon being honorable men; but if you were to hear the enormous lies they tell their slaves, you would have small respect for their veracity. I have spoken plain English. Pardon me. I cannot use a milder term. When they visit the north, and return home, they tell their slaves of the runaways they have seen, and describe them to be in the most deplorable condition. A slaveholder once told me that he had seen a runaway friend of mine in New York, and that she besought him to take her back to her master, for she was literally dying of starvation; that many days she had only one cold potato to eat, and at other times could get nothing at all. He said he refused to take her, because he knew her master would not thank him for bringing such a miserable wretch to his house. He ended by saying to me, "This is the punishment she brought on herself for running away from a kind master."

This whole story was false. I afterwards staid with that friend in New York, and found her in comfortable circumstances. She had never thought of such a thing as wishing to go back to slavery. Many of the slaves believe such stories, and think it is not worth while to exchange slavery for such a hard kind of freedom. It is difficult to persuade such that freedom could make them useful men, and enable them to protect their wives and children. If those heathen in our Christian land had as much teaching as some Hindoos, they would think otherwise. They would know that liberty is more valuable than life. They would begin to understand their own capabilities, and exert themselves to become men and women.

But while the Free States sustain a law which hurls fugitives back into slavery, how can the slaves resolve to become men? There are some who strive to protect wives and daughters from the insults of their masters; but those who have such sentiments have had advantages above the general mass of slaves. They have been partially civilized and Christianized by favorable circumstances. Some are bold enough to utter such sentiments to their masters. O, that there were more of them!

Some poor creatures have been so brutalized by the lash that they will sneak out of the way to give their masters free access to their wives and daughters. Do you think this proves the black man to belong to an inferior order of beings? What would you be, if you had been born and brought up a slave, with generations of slaves for ancestors? I admit that the black man is inferior. But what is it that makes him so? It is the ignorance in which white men compel him to live; it is the torturing whip that lashes manhood out of him; it is the fierce bloodhounds of the South, and the scarcely less cruel human bloodhounds of the north, who enforce the Fugitive Slave Law. They do the work.

Southern gentlemen indulge in the most contemptuous expressions about the Yankees, while they, on their part, consent to do the vilest work for them, such as the ferocious bloodhounds and the despised negro-hunters are employed to do at home. When southerners go to the north, they are proud to do them honor; but the northern man is not welcome south of Mason and Dixon's line, unless he suppresses every thought and feeling at variance with their "peculiar institution." Nor is it enough to be silent. The masters are not pleased, unless they obtain a greater degree of subservience than that; and they are generally accommodated. Do they respect the northerner for this? I trow not. Even the slaves despise "a northern man with southern principles;" and that is the class they generally see. When northerners go to the south to reside, they prove very apt scholars. They soon imbibe the sentiments and disposition of their neighbors, and generally go beyond their teachers. Of the two, they are proverbially the hardest masters.

They seem to satisfy their consciences with the doctrine that God created the Africans to be slaves. What a libel upon the heavenly Father, who "made of one blood all nations of men!" And then who are Africans? Who can measure the amount of Anglo-Saxon blood coursing in the veins of American slaves?

I have spoken of the pains slaveholders take to give their slaves a bad opinion of the north; but, notwithstanding this, intelligent slaves are aware that they have many friends in the Free States. Even the most ignorant have some confused notions about it. They knew that I could read; and I was often asked if I had seen any thing in the newspapers about white folks over in the big north, who were trying to get their freedom for them. Some believe that the abolitionists have already made them free, and that it is established by law, but that their masters prevent the law from going into effect. One woman begged me to get a newspaper and read it over. She said her husband told her that the black people had sent word to the queen of 'Merica that they were all slaves; that she didn't believe it, and went to Washington city to see the president about it. They quarrelled; she drew her sword upon him, and swore that he should help her to make them all free.

That poor, ignorant woman thought that America was governed by a Queen, to whom the President was subordinate. I wish the President was subordinate to Queen Justice.

CHAPTER NINE

Sketches Of Neighboring Slaveholders.

There was a planter in the country, not far from us, whom I will call Mr. Litch. He was an ill-bred, uneducated man, but very wealthy. He had six hundred slaves, many of whom he did not know by sight. His extensive plantation was managed by well-paid overseers. There was a jail and a whipping post on his grounds; and whatever cruelties were perpetrated there, they passed without comment. He was so effectually screened by his great wealth that he was called to no account for his crimes, not even for murder.

Various were the punishments resorted to. A favorite one was to tie a rope round a man's body, and suspend him from the ground. A fire was kindled over him, from which was suspended a piece of fat pork. As this cooked, the scalding drops of fat continually fell on the bare flesh. On his own plantation, he required very strict obedience to the eighth commandment. But depredations on the neighbors were allowable, provided the culprit managed to evade detection or suspicion. If a neighbor brought a charge of theft against any of his slaves, he was browbeaten by the master, who assured him that his slaves had enough of every thing at home, and had no inducement to steal. No sooner was the neighbor's back turned, than the accused was sought out, and whipped for his lack of discretion. If a slave stole from him even a pound of meat or a peck of corn, if detection followed, he was put in chains and imprisoned, and so kept till his form was attenuated by hunger and suffering.

A freshet once bore his wine cellar and meat house miles away from the plantation. Some slaves followed, and secured bits of meat and bottles of wine. Two were detected; a ham and some liquor being found in their huts. They were summoned by their master. No words were used, but a club felled them to the ground. A rough box was their coffin, and their interment was a dog's burial. Nothing was said.

Murder was so common on his plantation that he feared to be alone after nightfall. He might have believed in ghosts.

His brother, if not equal in wealth, was at least equal in cruelty. His bloodhounds were well trained. Their pen was spacious, and a terror to the slaves. They were let loose on a runaway, and, if they tracked him, they literally tore the flesh from his bones. When this slaveholder died, his shrieks and groans were so frightful that they appalled his own friends. His last words were, "I am going to hell; bury my money with me."

After death his eyes remained open. To press the lids down, silver dollars were laid on them. These were buried with him. From this circumstance, a rumor went abroad that his coffin was filled with money. Three times his grave was opened, and his coffin taken out. The last time, his body was found on the ground, and a flock of buzzards were pecking at it. He was again interred, and a sentinel set over his grave. The perpetrators were never discovered.

Cruelty is contagious in uncivilized communities. Mr. Conant, a neighbor of Mr. Litch, returned from town one evening in a partial state of intoxication. His body servant gave him some offence. He was divested of his clothes, except his shirt, whipped, and tied to a large tree in front of the house. It was a stormy night in winter. The wind blew bitterly cold, and the boughs of the old tree crackled under falling sleet. A member of the family, fearing he would freeze to death, begged that he might be taken down; but the master would not relent. He remained there three hours; and, when he was cut down, he was more dead than alive. Another slave, who stole a pig from this master, to appease his hunger, was terribly flogged. In desperation, he tried to run away. But at the end of two miles, he was so faint with loss of blood, he thought he was dying. He had a wife, and he longed to see her once more. Too sick to walk, he crept back that long distance on his hands and knees. When he reached his master's, it was night. He had not strength to rise and open the gate. He moaned, and tried to call for help. I had a friend living in the same family. At last his cry reached her. She went out and found the prostrate man at the gate. She ran back to the house for assistance, and two men returned with her. They carried him in, and laid him on the floor. The back of his shirt was one clot of blood. By means of lard, my friend loosened it from the raw flesh. She bandaged him, gave him cool drink, and left him to rest. The master said he deserved a hundred more lashes. When his own labor was stolen from him, he had stolen food to appease his hunger. This was his crime.

Another neighbor was a Mrs. Wade. At no hour of the day was there cessation of the lash on her premises. Her labors began with the dawn, and did not cease till long after nightfall. The barn was her particular place of torture. There she lashed the slaves with the might of a man. An old slave of hers once said to me, "It is hell in missis's house. 'Pears I can never get out. Day and night I prays to die."

The mistress died before the old woman, and, when dying, entreated her husband not to permit any one of her slaves to look on her after death. A slave who had nursed her children, and had still a child in her care, watched her chance, and stole with it in her arms to the room where lay her dead mistress. She gazed a while on her, then raised her hand and dealt two blows on her face, saying, as she did so, "The devil is got you now!" She forgot that the child was looking on. She had just begun to talk; and she said to her father, "I did see ma, and mammy did strike ma, so," striking her own face with her little hand. The master was startled. He could not imagine how the nurse could obtain access to the room where the corpse lay; for he kept the door locked. He questioned her. She confessed that what the child had said was true, and told how she had procured the key. She was sold to Georgia.

In my childhood I knew a valuable slave, named Charity, and loved her, as all children did. Her young mistress married, and took her to Louisiana. Her little boy, James, was sold to a good sort of master. He became involved in debt, and James was sold again to a wealthy slaveholder, noted for his cruelty. With this man he grew up to manhood, receiving the treatment of a dog. After a severe whipping, to save himself from further infliction of the lash, with which he was threatened, he took to the woods. He was in a most miserable condition—cut by the cowskin, half naked, half starved, and without the means of procuring a crust of bread.

Some weeks after his escape, he was captured, tied, and carried back to his master's plantation. This man considered punishment in his jail, on bread and water, after receiving hundreds of lashes, too mild for the poor slave's offence. Therefore he decided, after the overseer should have whipped him to his satisfaction, to have him placed between the screws of the cotton gin, to stay as long as he had been in the woods. This wretched creature was cut with the whip from his head to his feet, then washed with strong brine, to prevent the flesh from mortifying, and make it heal sooner than it otherwise would. He was then put into the cotton gin, which was screwed down, only allowing him room to turn on his side when he could not lie on his back. Every morning a slave was sent with a piece of bread and bowl of water, which were placed within reach of the poor fellow. The slave was charged, under penalty of severe punishment, not to speak to him.

Four days passed, and the slave continued to carry the bread and water. On the second morning, he found the bread gone, but the water untouched. When he had been in the press four days and five nights, the slave informed his master that the water had not been used for four mornings, and that a horrible stench came from the gin house. The overseer was sent to examine into it. When the press was unscrewed, the dead body was found partly eaten by rats and vermin. Perhaps the rats that devoured his bread had gnawed him before life was extinct. Poor Charity! Grandmother and I often asked each other how her affectionate heart would bear the news, if she should ever hear of the murder of her son. We had known her husband, and knew that James was like him in manliness and intelligence. These were the qualities that made it so hard for him to be a plantation slave. They put him into a rough box, and buried him with less feeling than would have been manifested for an old house dog. Nobody asked any questions. He was a slave; and the feeling was that the master had a right to do what he pleased with his own property. And what did he care for the value of a slave? He had hundreds of them. When they had finished their daily toil, they must hurry to eat their little morsels, and be ready to extinguish their pine knots before nine o'clock, when the overseer went his patrol rounds. He entered every cabin, to see that men and their wives had gone to bed together, lest the men, from over-fatigue, should fall asleep in the chimney corner, and remain there till the morning horn called them to their daily task. Women are considered of no value, unless they continually increase their owner's stock. They are put on a par with animals. This same master shot a woman through the head, who had run away and been brought back to him. No one called him to account for it. If a slave resisted being whipped, the bloodhounds were unpacked, and set upon him, to tear his flesh from his bones. The master who did these things was highly educated, and styled a perfect gentleman. He also boasted the name and standing of a Christian, though Satan never had a truer follower.

I could tell of more slaveholders as cruel as those I have described. They are not exceptions to the general rule. I do not say there are no humane slaveholders. Such characters do exist, notwithstanding the hardening influences around them. But they are "like angels' visits—few and far between."

I knew a young lady who was one of these rare specimens. She was an orphan, and inherited as slaves a woman and her six children. Their father was a free man. They had a comfortable home of their own, parents and children living together. The mother and eldest daughter served their mistress during the day, and at night returned to their dwelling, which was on the premises. The young lady was very pious, and there was some reality in her religion. She taught her slaves to lead pure lives, and wished them to enjoy the fruit of their own industry. Her religion was not a garb put on for Sunday, and laid aside till Sunday returned again. The eldest daughter of the slave mother was promised in marriage to a free man; and the day before the wedding this good mistress emancipated her, in order that her marriage might have the sanction of law.

Report said that this young lady cherished an unrequited affection for a man who had resolved to marry for wealth. In the course of time a rich uncle of hers died. He left six thousand dollars to his two sons by a colored woman, and the remainder of his property to this orphan niece. The metal soon attracted the magnet. The lady and her weighty purse became his. She offered to manumit her slaves—telling them that her marriage might make unexpected changes in their destiny, and she wished to insure their happiness. They refused to take their freedom, saying that she had always been their best friend, and they could not be so happy any where as with her. I was not surprised. I had often seen them in their comfortable home, and thought that the whole town did not contain a happier family. They had never felt slavery; and, when it was too late, they were convinced of its reality.

When the new master claimed this family as his property, the father became furious, and went to his mistress for protection. "I can do nothing for you now, Harry," said she. "I no longer have the power I had a week ago. I have succeeded in obtaining the freedom of your wife; but I cannot obtain it for your children." The unhappy father swore that nobody should take his children from him. He concealed them in the woods for some days; but they were discovered and taken. The father was put in jail, and the two oldest boys sold to Georgia. One little girl, too young to be of service to her master, was left with the wretched mother. The other three were carried to their master's plantation. The eldest soon became a mother, and, when the slaveholder's wife looked at the babe, she wept bitterly. She knew that her own husband had violated the purity she had so carefully inculcated. She had a second child by her master, and then he sold her and his offspring to his brother. She bore two children to the brother, and was sold again. The next sister went crazy. The life she was compelled to lead drove her mad. The third one became the mother of five daughters. Before the birth of the fourth the pious mistress died. To the last, she rendered every kindness to the slaves that her unfortunate circumstances permitted. She passed away peacefully, glad to close her eyes on a life which had been made so wretched by the man she loved.

This man squandered the fortune he had received, and sought to retrieve his affairs by a second marriage; but, having retired after a night of drunken debauch, he was found dead in the morning. He was called a good master; for he fed and clothed his slaves better than most masters, and the lash was not heard on his plantation so frequently as on many others. Had it not been for slavery, he would have been a better man, and his wife a happier woman.

No pen can give an adequate description of the all-pervading corruption produced by slavery. The slave girl is reared in an atmosphere of licentiousness and fear. The lash and the foul talk of her master and his sons are her teachers. When she is fourteen or fifteen, her owner, or his sons, or the overseer, or perhaps all of them, begin to bribe her with presents. If these fail to accomplish their purpose, she is whipped or starved into submission to their will. She may have had religious principles inculcated by some pious mother or grandmother, or some good mistress; she may have a lover, whose good opinion and peace of mind are dear to her heart; or the profligate men who have power over her may be exceedingly odious to her. But resistance is hopeless.

"The poor worm
Shall prove her contest vain. Life's little day
Shall pass, and she is gone!"

The slaveholder's sons are, of course, vitiated, even while boys, by the unclean influences every where around them. Nor do the master's daughters always escape. Severe retributions sometimes come upon him for the wrongs he does to the daughters of the slaves. The white daughters early hear their parents quarrelling about some female slave. Their curiosity is excited, and they soon learn the cause. They are attended by the young slave girls whom their father has corrupted; and they hear such talk as should never meet youthful ears, or any other ears. They know that the women slaves are subject to their father's authority in all things; and in some cases they exercise the same authority over the men slaves. I have myself seen the master of such a household whose head was bowed down in shame; for it was known in the neighborhood that his daughter had selected one of the meanest slaves on his plantation to be the father of his first grandchild. She did not make her advances to her equals, nor even to her father's more intelligent servants. She selected the most brutalized, over whom her authority could be exercised with less fear of exposure. Her father, half frantic with rage, sought to revenge himself on the offending black man; but his daughter, foreseeing the storm that would arise, had given him free papers, and sent him out of the state.

In such cases the infant is smothered, or sent where it is never seen by any who know its history. But if the white parent is the father, instead of the mother, the offspring are unblushingly reared for the market. If they are girls, I have indicated plainly enough what will be their inevitable destiny.

You may believe what I say; for I write only that whereof I know. I was twenty-one years in that cage of obscene birds. I can testify, from my own experience and observation, that slavery is a curse to the whites as well as to the blacks. It makes the white fathers cruel and sensual; the sons violent and licentious; it contaminates the daughters, and makes the wives wretched. And as for the colored race, it needs an abler pen than mine to describe the extremity of their sufferings, the depth of their degradation.

Yet few slaveholders seem to be aware of the widespread moral ruin occasioned by this wicked system. Their talk is of blighted cotton crops—not of the blight on their children's souls.

If you want to be fully convinced of the abominations of slavery, go on a southern plantation, and call yourself a negro trader. Then there will be no concealment; and you will see and hear things that will seem to you impossible among human beings with immortal souls.

A Perilous Passage In The Slave Girl's Life.

After my lover went away, Dr. Flint contrived a new plan. He seemed to have an idea that my fear of my mistress was his greatest obstacle. In the blandest tones, he told me that he was going to build a small house for me, in a secluded place, four miles away from the town. I shuddered; but I was constrained to listen, while he talked of his intention to give me a home of my own, and to make a lady of me. Hitherto, I had escaped my dreaded fate, by being in the midst of people. My grandmother had already had high words with my master about me. She had told him pretty plainly what she thought of his character, and there was considerable gossip in the neighborhood about our affairs, to which the open-mouthed jealousy of Mrs. Flint contributed not a little. When my master said he was going to build a house for me, and that he could do it with little trouble and expense, I was in hopes something would happen to frustrate his scheme; but I soon heard that the house was actually begun. I vowed before my Maker that I would never enter it. I had rather toil on the plantation from dawn till dark; I had rather live and die in jail, than drag on, from day to day, through such a living death. I was determined that the master, whom I so hated and loathed, who had blighted the prospects of my youth, and made my life a desert, should not, after my long struggle with him, succeed at last in trampling his victim under his feet. I would do any thing, every thing, for the sake of defeating him. What could I do? I thought and thought, till I became desperate, and made a plunge into the abyss.

And now, reader, I come to a period in my unhappy life, which I would gladly forget if I could. The remembrance fills me with sorrow and shame. It pains me to tell you of it; but I have promised to tell you the truth, and I will do it honestly, let it cost me what it may. I will not try to screen myself behind the plea of compulsion from a master; for it was not so. Neither can I plead ignorance or thoughtlessness. For years, my master had done his utmost to pollute my mind with foul images, and to destroy the pure principles inculcated by my grandmother, and the good mistress of my childhood. The influences of slavery had had the same effect on me that they had on other young girls; they had made me prematurely knowing, concerning the evil ways of the world. I knew what I did, and I did it with deliberate calculation.

But, O, ye happy women, whose purity has been sheltered from childhood, who have been free to choose the objects of your affection, whose homes are protected by law, do not judge the poor desolate slave girl too severely! If slavery had been abolished, I, also, could have married the man of my choice; I could have had a home shielded by the laws; and I should have been spared the painful task of confessing what I am now about to relate; but all my prospects had been blighted by slavery. I wanted to keep myself pure; and, under the most adverse circumstances, I tried hard to preserve my self-respect; but I was struggling alone in the powerful grasp of the demon Slavery; and the monster proved too strong for me. I felt as if I was forsaken by God and man; as if all my efforts must be frustrated; and I became reckless in my despair.

I have told you that Dr. Flint's persecutions and his wife's jealousy had given rise to some gossip in the neighborhood. Among others, it chanced that a white unmarried gentleman had obtained some knowledge of the circumstances in which I was placed. He knew my grandmother, and often spoke to me in the street. He became interested for me, and asked questions about my master, which I answered in part. He expressed a great deal of sympathy, and a wish to aid me. He constantly sought opportunities to see me, and wrote to me frequently. I was a poor slave girl, only fifteen years old.

So much attention from a superior person was, of course, flattering; for human nature is the same in all. I also felt grateful for his sympathy, and encouraged by his kind words. It seemed to me a great thing to have such a friend. By degrees, a more tender feeling crept into my heart. He was an educated and eloquent gentleman; too eloquent, alas, for the poor slave girl who trusted in him. Of course I saw whither all this was tending. I knew the impassable gulf between us; but to be an object of interest to a man who is not married, and who is not her master, is agreeable to the pride and feelings of a slave, if her miserable situation has left her any pride or sentiment. It seems less degrading to give one's self, than to submit to compulsion. There is something akin to freedom in having a lover who has no control over you, except that which he gains by kindness and attachment. A master may treat you as rudely as he pleases, and you dare not speak; moreover, the wrong does not seem so great with an unmarried man, as with one who has a wife to be made unhappy. There may be sophistry in all this; but the condition of a slave confuses all principles of morality, and, in fact, renders the practice of them impossible.

When I found that my master had actually begun to build the lonely cottage, other feelings mixed with those I have described. Revenge, and calculations of interest, were added to flattered vanity and sincere gratitude for kindness. I knew nothing would enrage Dr. Flint so much as to know that I favored another; and it was something to triumph over my tyrant even in that small way. I thought he would revenge himself by selling me, and I was sure my friend, Mr. Sands, would buy me. He was a man of more generosity and feeling than my master, and I thought my freedom could be easily obtained from him. The crisis of my fate now came so near that I was desperate. I shuddered to think of being the mother of children that should be owned by my old tyrant. I knew that as soon as a new fancy took him, his victims were sold far off to get rid of them; especially if they had children. I had seen several women sold, with his babies at the breast. He never allowed his offspring by slaves to remain long in sight of himself and his wife. Of a man who was not my master I could ask to have my children well supported; and in this case, I felt confident I should obtain the boon. I also felt quite sure that they would be made free. With all these thoughts revolving in my mind, and seeing no other way of escaping the doom I so much dreaded, I made a headlong plunge. Pity me, and pardon me, O virtuous reader! You never knew what it is to be a slave; to be entirely unprotected by law or custom; to have the laws reduce you to the condition of a chattel, entirely subject to the will of another. You never exhausted your ingenuity in avoiding the snares, and eluding the power of a hated tyrant; you never shuddered at the sound of his footsteps, and trembled within hearing of his voice. I know I did wrong. No one can feel it more sensibly than I do. The painful and humiliating memory will haunt me to my dying day. Still, in looking back, calmly, on the events of my life, I feel that the slave woman ought not to be judged by the same standard as others.

The months passed on. I had many unhappy hours. I secretly mourned over the sorrow I was bringing on my grandmother, who had so tried to shield me from harm. I knew that I was the greatest comfort of her old age, and that it was a source of pride to her that I had not degraded myself, like most of the slaves. I wanted to confess to her that I was no longer worthy of her love; but I could not utter the dreaded words.

As for Dr. Flint, I had a feeling of satisfaction and triumph in the thought of telling him. From time to time he told me of his intended arrangements, and I was silent. At last, he came and told me the cottage was completed, and ordered me to go to it. I told him I would never enter it. He said, "I have heard enough of such talk as that. You shall go, if you are carried by force; and you shall remain there."

I replied, "I will never go there. In a few months I shall be a mother."

He stood and looked at me in dumb amazement, and left the house without a word. I thought I should be happy in my triumph over him. But now that the truth was out, and my relatives would hear of it, I felt wretched. Humble as were their circumstances, they had pride in my good character. Now, how could I look them in the face? My self-respect was gone! I had resolved that I would be virtuous, though I was a slave. I had said, "Let the storm beat! I will brave it till I die." And now, how humiliated I felt!

I went to my grandmother. My lips moved to make confession, but the words stuck in my throat. I sat down in the shade of a tree at her door and began to sew. I think she saw something unusual was the matter with me. The mother of slaves is very watchful. She knows there is no security for her children. After they have entered their teens she lives in daily expectation of trouble. This leads to many questions. If the girl is of a sensitive nature, timidity keeps her from answering truthfully, and this well-meant course has a tendency to drive her from maternal counsels. Presently, in came my mistress, like a mad woman, and accused me concerning her husband. My grandmother, whose suspicions had been previously awakened, believed what she said. She exclaimed, "O Linda! has it come to this? I had rather see you dead than to see you as you now are. You are a disgrace to your dead mother." She tore from my fingers my mother's wedding ring and her silver thimble. "Go away!" she exclaimed, "and never come to my house, again." Her reproaches fell so hot and heavy, that they left me no chance to answer. Bitter tears, such as the eyes never shed but once, were my only answer. I rose from my seat, but fell back again, sobbing. She did not speak to me; but the tears were running down her furrowed cheeks, and they scorched me like fire. She had always been so kind to me! So kind! How I longed to throw myself at her feet, and tell her all the truth! But she had ordered me to go, and never to come there again. After a few minutes, I mustered strength, and started to obey her. With what feelings did I now close that little gate, which I used to open with such an eager hand in my childhood! It closed upon me with a sound I never heard before.

Where could I go? I was afraid to return to my master's. I walked on recklessly, not caring where I went, or what would become of me. When I had gone four or five miles, fatigue compelled me to stop. I sat down on the stump of an old tree. The stars were shining through the boughs above me. How they mocked me, with their bright, calm light! The hours passed by, and as I sat there alone a chilliness and deadly sickness came over me. I sank on the ground. My mind was full of horrid thoughts. I prayed to die; but the prayer was not answered. At last, with great effort I roused myself, and walked some distance further, to the house of a woman who had been a friend of my mother. When I told her why I was there, she spoke soothingly to me; but I could not be comforted. I thought I could bear my shame if I could only be reconciled to my grandmother. I longed to open my heart to her. I thought if she could know the real state of the case, and all I had been bearing for years, she would perhaps judge me less harshly. My friend advised me to send for her. I did so; but days of agonizing suspense passed before she came. Had she utterly forsaken me? No. She came at last. I knelt before her, and told her the things that had poisoned my life; how long I had been persecuted; that I saw no way of escape; and in an hour of extremity I had become desperate. She listened in silence. I told her I would bear any thing and do any thing, if in time I had hopes of obtaining her forgiveness. I begged of her to pity me, for my dead mother's sake. And she did pity me. She did not say, "I forgive you;" but she looked at me lovingly, with her eyes full of tears. She laid her old hand gently on my head, and murmured, "Poor child! Poor child!"

www.ingramcontent.com/pod-product-compliance
Lightning Source LLC
Chambersburg PA
CBHW031324130726
47988CB00007B/2968